SOMETIMES I WISH

All inquiries should be addressed to:
Barron's Educational Series, Inc.
250 Wireless Boulevard
Hauppauge, NY 11788

International Standard Book Number: 0-8120-4681-1

Library of Congress Catalog Card Number: 91-3119

Library of Congress Cataloging-in-Publication Data

Erickson, Gina Clegg.
    Sometimes I wish / Gina Clegg Erickson and Kelli C. Foster :
illustrations by Kerri Gifford.
        p.   cm. — (Get ready...get set...read!)
Summary: Trish the fish and Jim the bird enjoy swimming and
flying but sometimes wish they could exchange places.
        ISBN 0-8120-4681-3
        (1. Fishes—Fiction. 2. Birds—Fiction. 3. Identity—Fiction.
4. Stories in rhyme.) I. Foster, Kelli C. II. Gifford, Kerri, ill. III. Title.
IV. Series: Erickson, Gina Clegg. Get ready...get set...read!
PZ8.3.E787So   1991
(E)—dc20   91-3119
                                                        CIP
                                                        AC

PRINTED IN HONG KONG
19

GET READY...GET SET...READ!

SOMETIMES I WISH

by
Foster & Erickson

Illustrations by
Kerri Gifford

BARRON'S

My name is Trish.

I am a fish in a dish.

All day long

I swish, swish, swish.

Sometimes I wish

I could fly...

...like him.

My name is Jim.

Flying keeps me

slim and trim.

I like to sit upon the rim

of Trish's dish to see her swim.

Sometimes I wish

I could swim like Trish.

Sometimes...
wishes come true.

The End

The ISH Word Family

fish
dish
wish
wishes
Trish
swish

The IM Word Family

him
Jim
rim
slim
trim
swim

Sight Words

a
of
to
my
flying
all
her
the
come
could
sometimes

Dear Parents and Educators:

Welcome to *Get Ready...Get Set...Read!*

We've created these books to introduce children to the magic of reading.

Each story in the series is built around one or two word families. For example, *A Mop for Pop* uses the OP word family. Letters and letter blends are added to OP to form words such as TOP, LOP, and STOP. As you can see, once children are able to read OP, it is a simple task for them to read the entire word family. In addition to word families, we have used a limited number of "sight words." These are words found to occur with high frequency in the books your child will soon be reading. Being able to identify sight words greatly increases reading skill.

You might find the steps outlined on the facing page useful in guiding your work with your beginning reader.

We had great fun creating these books, and great pleasure sharing them with our children. We hope *Get Ready...Get Set...Read!* helps make this first step in reading fun for you and your new reader.

Kelli C. Foster, PhD
Educational Psychologist

Gina Clegg Erickson, MA
Reading Specialist